Reading Together

THE TRUE STORY OF
HUMPTY DUMPTY

Read it together

The True Story of Humpty Dumpty is a playful version of a favourite nursery rhyme. Children who know the rhyme well will recognize the jokes and make connections with the original.

I know this story.

The repeated words and phrases within the story encourage children to join in the reading. You can make it into a rhyming game by leaving space for children to think of the matching word or phrase.

Humpty Dumpty laughed. "Oh dear," he said, "you've ...

hurt your ear."

Then he wobbled and wobbled and fell down.

With books they know well, children can have a go at reading to you. With time and practice their readings will get closer to the words on the page. Praising their early attempts, rather than jumping in to correct them, helps to build their confidence.

Help children to guess if they get stuck on a word. With this book the pictures tell the story in detail, so search through them for clues.

Can you stand on one leg and jug—

What does he do with the bricks?

Juggle? ...juggle with bricks.

Rhymes help children to look closely at words and notice patterns in the way they look and sound.

Those words look the same.

Which letters are different?

Then he wobbled and wobbled, and then he fell off.

Humpty Dumpty laughed. "Tee hee," he said, "you've l— your l—."

This is funnier than the other Humpty Dumpty.

Show me a funny bit.

Talking about books is part of being a reader. Children might ask you questions and give their opinion about this particular *Humpty Dumpty*. You can help them to make links with other books or rhymes they know.

We hope you enjoy reading this book together.

First published 1987 by Walker Books Ltd
87 Vauxhall Walk, London SE11 5HJ

This edition produced 2002 for
The Book People Ltd, Hall Wood Avenue,
Haydock, St Helens WA11 9UL

2 4 6 8 10 9 7 5 3 1

Text © 1987 Sarah Hayes
Illustrations © 1987 Charlotte Voake
Introductory and concluding notes © 1998 CLPE/LB Southwark

Printed in Hong Kong

ISBN 0-7445-5702-X

THE TRUE STORY OF
HUMPTY DUMPTY

Sarah Hayes   Charlotte Voake

TED SMART

Humpty Dumpty sat on a wall.
A horse came up to watch.
"Can you sit on this wall, horse?"
Humpty Dumpty said.

"Of course," said the horse.
And he did.

Then he wobbled and wobbled,
and then he fell off.

Humpty Dumpty laughed.
"Tee-hee," he said,
"you've hurt your knee."

Humpty Dumpty sat on the wall.
Another horse came up to watch.
"Can you stand on this wall, horse?"
Humpty Dumpty said.

"Of course," said the horse.
And he did.

Then he wobbled and wobbled,
and then he fell off.

Humpty Dumpty laughed.
"Oh dear," he said,
"you've hurt your ear."

Humpty Dumpty sat on the wall.
A man came up to watch.
"Can you stand on one leg
on this wall, man?"
Humpty Dumpty said.

"Yes," said the man, "I can."
And he did.

Then he wobbled and wobbled,
and then he fell off.

Humpty Dumpty laughed.
"Ho-ho," he said,
"you've hurt your toe."

Humpty Dumpty sat on the wall.
Another man came up to watch.
"Can you stand on one leg
and juggle with bricks
on this wall, man?"
Humpty Dumpty said.

"Well," said the man,
"I think I can."
And he did.

Then he wobbled and wobbled,
and then he fell off.

Humpty Dumpty laughed.
"Go to bed," he said,
"you've hurt your head."

Humpty Dumpty sat on the wall.
The King came up to watch.
He saw his horses
and he saw his men.

And the King was terribly,
terribly cross.

"Come down," the King said.
"Come down from that wall."
But Humpty Dumpty said nothing at all.
He stood on one leg and juggled with bricks.
He did cartwheels and headstands
and all sorts of tricks.

Then he wobbled and wobbled,
and then he fell off.
CRASH!

And all the King's horses,

and all the King's men ...

put Humpty Dumpty together again.
And Humpty said, "After such a great fall
I'll never ever climb back on that wall."

But he did!

Read it again

The true story?

A good way to help children see the jokes in *The True Story of Humpty Dumpty* is to read them the original rhyme. What differences do they notice?

Atishoo!

Atishoo!

We all hop about.

*Humpty Dumpty
sat on a wall,
Humpty Dumpty
had a great fall.
All the King's horses and
All the King's men,
Couldn't put Humpty
together again.*

Different endings

This story changes a well-known rhyme and has a different ending. You could make up your own endings to other familiar rhymes such as *Jack and Jill, Little Jack Horner, Ring-a-Ring-o'-Roses* and *Hey Diddle, Diddle.*

Talking pictures

Using the pictures in the book, children can retell the story in their own words.

The horse sat on the wall and ate some of Humpty Dumpty's cakes.

Humpty Dumpty sat on a wall. A horse came up to watch. "Can you sit on this wall, horse?" Humpty Dumpty said.

"Of course," said the horse. And he did.

Then he wobbled and wobbled, and then he fell off.

Act it out

The story is a good one to act out using toys or puppets with an imaginary wall such as a chair seat or an upturned box.

"Come down," the King said.

CRASH!

Make a tape

You can read the book together and make a tape of it for your child to play back with the book.

The King came up to watch...

umpty Dumpty laughed.
ee-hee," he said.
ou've hurt your knee."

The horse fell off and Humpty Dumpty laughed at him. The horse was crying.

Different versions

There are lots of different versions of *Humpty Dumpty* you could find in nursery rhyme collections and in stories like these. Look out for *Once Upon a Time* – another *Reading Together* story – which includes Humpty Dumpty and other familiar characters, such as the three bears and Little Red Riding Hood.